For my mum

First published 2019 by Walker Books Ltd
87 Vauxhall Walk, London SE11 5HJ

10 9 8 7 6 5 4 3 2 1

© 2019 Polly Dunbar

The right of Polly Dunbar to be identified as author/illustrator of this work has been asserted by her in accordance with the Copyright, Designs and Patents Act 1988

This book has been typeset in Burbank Big Regular

Printed in China

British Library Cataloguing in Publication Data: a catalogue record for this book is available from the British Library

ISBN 978-1-4063-7696-8

www.walker.co.uk

WALKER BOOKS
AND SUBSIDIARIES
LONDON · BOSTON · SYDNEY · AUCKLAND

Red

by Polly Dunbar

Look!
I spy the biscuit jar.
I'll get it down,
It's not *too* far.

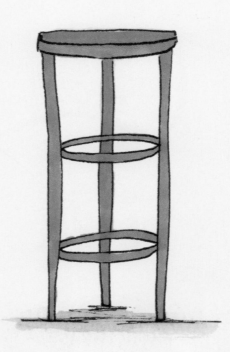

If I just climb ...
stretch ... reach
and jump...

Nearly ... nearly...

"Oh, little one!" says my mum.
"You've banged your head,
that's not much fun."

Yes! I had a bump.
It made me cry.
The biscuit jar
was up too high!

**My socks
are
down.**

**My pants
are
twisted.**

I want...

I want...

I WANT

A BISCUIT!

Put me down!
Don't stroke my hair.
I want a *biscuit*,
don't you care?

**The lid is on.
And I'm not strong.**

**Everything is
wrong,
wrong,
WRONG!**

Raaah!

I scream.

Graaah!

I roar.

Wump-Wump waa-waa!

I hit the floor.

Watch me while
I bang my head!

'Cause now
I'm seeing ...

RED!
RED!
RED!

"Oh, Little One," says my mum.
Please don't scream,
please don't roar.
It doesn't help to hit the floor.
I know you're seeing
red, red, red,
But why not
count to
10
instead?

"Start with
1
then
2
then
3.
You can do it,
count with me."

2

two

3

three

4
four

5
five

6
six

7

seven

8

eight

9

nine

10

ten

And then ...

breathe.

phew-eeeeeee.

Look!
My socks are up.

My pants un-twisted.

It must be time
to eat
that biscuit.

A little nibble.
A tiny bite.

Let's see if I can
get this right..

7, 8, 9 ... wow!

There's only one
more bite to come.
And look, my biscuit is
nom ... nom ...

Gone!

But that's OK.

One more for me, and one for you.
My mum says,
"Ma mwah moo."

And I say ...

"I Love you, too."